Serious Henry Meets Little Ricky

A Series About Wise Choices

By ARLENE STEIN

Illustrations by Hatice Bayramoglu

Serious Henry Meets Little Ricky

A Series About Wise Choices

Book 1

Published by Adriel Publishing

www.adrielpublishing.com

FIRST EDITION

Printed in the U.S.A.

Illustrations by Hatice Bayramoğlu

ISBN: 978-1-892324-29-0

DEDICATION

My Serious Henry series is dedicated to my father,

Abe Goldstein,

who proudly shared with anyone who would look,

the curriculum texts I wrote during my education career.

FOREWORD

Serious Henry and Little Ricky were created to represent the personification of my beloved pets. I, like other pet owners, bestow human characteristics on our little fur people. I hope children of young ages can enjoy the adventures that Serious Henry and Little Ricky experience in their everyday world.

Serious Henry is a serious chap.

Seriously kids,
Serious Henry is seriously serious about
everything serious.

Serious Henry is serious about his studying.
He wants to make good grades
so he can go to college.

Serious Henry is serious about safety.

He wants to be safe in everything he does.

Serious Henry is serious about

being a good friend to everyone he meets.

Serious Henry is serious about

everything serious.

One afternoon, Serious Henry saw a moving truck
down the street.

"Mommy, someone is moving into the new house.
May I go down the street to meet the family?
Maybe, I will have someone to go play with at the playground."

"Sure, Serious Henry. Be home by 5:00 in time for dinner."

Serious Henry ran down the street to see who was moving into the new house.

Serious Henry saw a little dog.

He walked up to the little dog.

"Hi, my name is Serious Henry. Who are you?"

"Hi, Serious Henry, my name is Ricky."

"It is so nice to meet you, Ricky.

We can be friends."

"Oh, thank you, Serious Henry, I would like to be friends

with you."

"Oh, look, Serious Henry, here comes my mommy."

"Hi, Ms. Ricky's mommy. My name is Serious Henry. I want to be Ricky's friend. It is very nice to meet you. Welcome to the neighborhood."

"Serious Henry, I am glad to meet you. I am happy that Ricky has a new friend with such nice manners."

"Ms. Ricky's mommy, I am serious about having nice manners. It is important to be polite to everyone. I want to treat everyone just like I would want my friends to treat me."

"Serious Henry, that is very nice. You will be a good friend for my little Ricky."

"Little Ricky, I like that name. Ricky, can I call you Little Ricky?"

"Sure, Serious Henry. My mommy calls me Little Ricky all of the time."

"Great. I love the name Little Ricky. Little Ricky, I want you to be my very best friend."

"Oh, Serious Henry, thank you. I want you to be my best friend too."

"Little Ricky, ask your mommy if you can go play with me at the playground down the street."

"Serious Henry, it is fine, let's go."

"No, Little Ricky. You must always ask your mommy or daddy before you go somewhere."

"Oh, Serious Henry, I am sure it is ok."

"No, Little Ricky. We must be serious about always letting our parents know we are leaving. We do not want them to be scared if they do not see us."

"OK, Serious Henry. That is a good idea. You are right."

"Mommy, may I go down to the playground to play with my new friend, Serious Henry?"

"Yes, Little Ricky. Stay with Serious Henry.

Come home soon."

Serious Henry and Little Ricky ran down to the playground.

Serious Henry showed Little Ricky the swings and sliding board. They played and played.

Serious Henry looked at his watch. It was late in the afternoon.

"Little Ricky, it is time to go. I told my mommy that I would be home by 5:00 for dinner."

"Oh, Serious Henry. I am having so much fun. Do we have to leave?"

"Yes, Little Ricky. I am serious about doing what my mommy tells me."

"OK, Serious Henry. You are a very good boy. Let's go home.

My mommy did tell me to come home soon. I need to be like you. I need to be serious about doing what my mommy tells me."

Serious Henry and Little Ricky walked down the street to their homes.

"Bye, bye, Little Ricky. I am so glad that you moved into my neighborhood. You are my new best friend."

Serious Henry patted Little Ricky on the back.

"Thank you Serious Henry, you are my new best friend, too."

"Little Ricky, I look forward to all of the fun
we will have. I will see you tomorrow."

"Bye, Serious Henry, see you tomorrow."

"Mommy, I'm home. I have a new friend. His name is Little Ricky."

"I am so glad you made a new friend, Serious Henry. You are a good boy. I hope you and your friend, Little Ricky, will have many good times together."

"Oh, mommy, I am sure we will. I can't wait for our next adventure. I know Little Ricky will be the very best friend I have ever had. He is serious about being a good boy just like me."

Serious Henry is a serious chap.

Seriously kids,
Serious Henry is seriously serious about
everything serious.

Author Arlene G. Stein

Arlene Stein graduated from the University of Texas at Austin with a degree in deaf education. Her masters degree is from the University of North Texas with a major in educational administration and a minor in special education. During her education career with the Dallas Independent School District, she worked as a teacher of the deaf, writer of curriculum and student texts, and special education administrator. Her writing and consequently awarding of state and federal educational grants provided the impetus for her love of both technical and creative writing. Through these grants, high interest, low reading level texts were produced for deaf students throughout the State of Texas. Stein's knowledge of curriculum elevated her work to a broader spectrum the latter part of her career where she served as a director of specialized services within the special education department. Upon retirement, Arlene's love of creative writing in the work force transcended to a new career in the writing of children's books. Her ideas for the "Serious Henry Series" came from the frolicking and exuberant personalities of her beloved pets, Henry and Ricky. To book Arlene to speak email: arlene@SeriousHenryBooks.com.

Made in the USA
Lexington, KY
18 November 2019

57206020R00029